To my nephew, Caleb.
You inspire me every day to keep soaring.

ISBN: 978-0-9977543-1-5

Library of Congress Control Number: 2018932758

Printed and manufactured in Melrose Park, Illinois

For information on booking the author for an appearance or speaking
engagement, contact Bantry Bay Media: bantrybaymedia@gmail.com.

Published by Bantry Bay Publishing, Chicago, Illinois
www.bantrybaybooks.com

The Journey of NEM

Written by Erika Brannock
Illustrated by John F. Baker III

BANTRY BAY PUBLISHING

CHICAGO

Dear Reader,

The Story of NEM is based on a true story — the story of my experience after attending the 2013 Boston Marathon.

It was a glorious day in Boston. The weather was sunny and just right — not too warm for the runners, not too chilly for the spectators. The city had an electrifying energy of optimism and joy.

My mother, Carol Downing, was running the marathon. My sister, Nicole, her husband, Michael, and I found a prime spot on Boylston Street near the finish line, ready to witness the completion of her amazing accomplishment.

As other spectators shifted and came and went, we edged closer to the fence separating all of us from the street. Eventually, we were at the front of a cheering crowd several rows deep on the sidewalk.

It was just so happy!

And then ...

I didn't actually hear the bomb go off, because my eardrums were blown out instantly. But I remember this whomping noise, and smoke, and flashes of yellow and orange, and then I was falling backwards slowly. Then I blacked out for a few seconds.

One of the joys of my life is teaching and caring for preschoolers. Above, I'm reading to some of my students at Davenport Preschool in Towson, Maryland.

When I came to, my first thought was, "No, this is not happening," and I closed my eyes. I had a conversation with God. I said, "You are not taking me yet. I'm not done. I'm not leaving."

Fifty days and 11 surgeries later, I left my "Boston family" — including the incredible nurses, doctors and staff at Beth Israel Deaconess Hospital — to resume my life, which had become starkly different with challenges I had never expected to face.

Gratitude and grace assumed new positions of strength in my life, and to try to list all of those who've helped me on my journey would fill this book and many more. Instead, along with the beautiful illustrations by John Baker, I wrote this book hoping to help children understand that when a hard thing happens to them, it's not going to defeat them; to understand that it's OK to be different, because we are all different in our own ways. Our main character, a dragonfly named NEM (Nicole, Erika, Michael), represents perseverance and strength, and guides the reader through adversity to a happy ending.

XO,
Erika

NEM was just an ordinary dragonfly.

At least, that's how she thought of herself.

She loved her family and friends, and they loved her back.

One day, NEM was enjoying a celebration in town with her family.

The day was a happy one, and she loved every minute of it. Life could not get any better.

Suddenly, a huge storm came and threw her against the largest tree in town.

NEM quickly found herself
alone and scared.

The next thing she saw was her mother's face looking down at her.

Right away, she felt safe.

But she knew something was different now.

"Mama, what happened?"
NEM asked.
"You're OK, NEM. That's the most important thing to remember," her mother told her.

"But part of your wing is missing now, sweetheart, and you are in a hospital."

NEM stayed in the hospital a long time while she got better.

While at the hospital, NEM had felt like she was at home with friends.

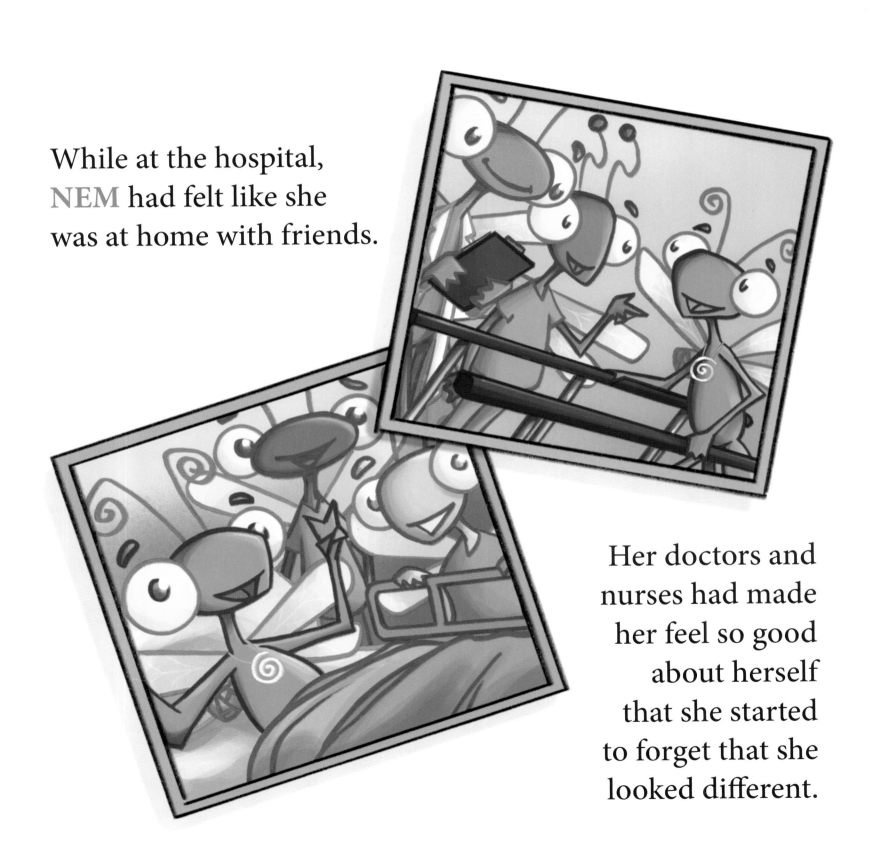

Her doctors and nurses had made her feel so good about herself that she started to forget that she looked different.

Because she had become friends with everyone in the hospital, it made it very hard for her to leave and go home.

What was going to happen when she left the hospital?

She knew that she was different from all the other dragonflies now.

"Mom, what if the other dragonflies think I'm weird-looking?" NEM asked.

"You're not weird-looking at all, my sweet girl. You just look a little different from the other dragonflies," her mother said.

The day finally came when it was time for NEM to leave the hospital. She was so nervous her stomach was twisted in a triple knot.

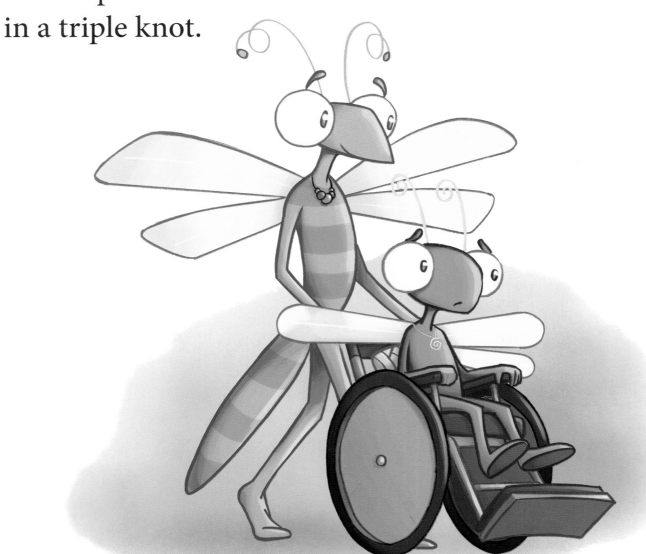

"OK, here goes. Just do it," NEM told herself as her mother pushed her wheelchair out of her hospital room.

As soon as NEM turned the corner to go down the hall, she was completely shocked by what she saw.

Everyone who had taken care of her in the hospital lined the hallway. They cheered NEM on as her mother pushed her toward the door.

NEM left the hospital with a huge smile on her face. She felt ready to conquer whatever came next.

A few days after being home, NEM met some of her friends for lunch. As NEM went up to the restaurant, her stomach started to hurt. But the pain went away almost as soon as she saw her friends.

They smiled at her just like they did before she lost part of her wing, and hugged her the same way — just more gently. They worried they would hurt NEM by hugging her too tightly.

As they sat and talked, NEM noticed that other dragonflies that flew by looked at her, but were not scared of her.

The little dragonflies were not scared and no one flew away.

No one pointed at her and whispered.

She wasn't that different from everyone else.

Although **NEM** didn't feel like people thought she was weird any more, she still had many struggles.
She had to wait to get her new wing and couldn't fly like other dragonflies, so it took her longer to get places.

NEM felt bad that her friends always had to wait for her.

At last, NEM got her new wing that was going to help her fly again. Her doctors told her it was called a prosthetic.

Everyone wanted to touch it. Everyone thought it was the coolest thing they'd ever seen.

NEM realized there was something very special about her now. Just because she was a little different, that was not a bad or scary thing.

She started to notice that all of the dragonflies were a little different in their own ways, and that made them special.

NEM began to tell herself every day: "We are all different and that is OK. It makes us special."

About the Author

Until 2:49 on the afternoon of April 15, 2013, Erika Brannock led the quiet life of a preschool teacher in Towson, Maryland, working on a master's degree in early childhood education. Everything changed when a bomb exploded at the Boston Marathon finish line, and she was rushed to Beth Israel Deaconess Medical Center where teams of doctors and nurses saved her life, but could not save her left leg. They amputated above the knee, and did their best to repair major damage to her right ankle, as well. After 50 days in the hospital and multiple surgeries, Erika was able to return home to Baltimore. In the months that followed, she endured 12 additional surgeries to repair her many injuries. With an indomitable spirit and determined optimism, Erika battled through setbacks, grueling rehab, and learned to walk with a prosthetic leg. She adapted to her "new normal," and resumed doing what she loves most: teaching preschoolers.

Erika is often asked to share her inspiring story and has given many presentations at high schools, hospitals, on television, and in a Towson University TEDx talk. She is eager to spread her messages about the healing powers of positive thinking and gratitude, and, as she now stresses to her preschoolers, the importance of accepting others as they are and celebrating our differences.

About the Illustrator

John F. Baker III is an illustrator, exhibit designer, and part-time failed ninja. He has worked in the Commercial Arts for over two decades, doing everything from advertising to cartooning to designing holiday decor. He has been dear friends with Erika for years, and is so proud to be able to be a part of bringing this story to life. He lives in Baltimore, Maryland, with his goofball wife, Sally, and their goofball son, Henry.

Underwriting assistance provided by

DANKMEYER
PROSTHETICS & ORTHOTICS

Experience The Dankmeyer Difference.
We are committed to enriching the lives of all those in the communities we serve.
Please call us today to find out how we can help enrich yours.

Toll Free: (800) 879-1245   Main Office: (410) 636-8114   Fax: (410) 636-8325
Email: info@dankmeyer.com

For more information on support organizations and Erika's journey, please visit:

The Amputee Coalition of America: www.amputee-coalition.org
No Limits Foundation: www.nolimitsfoundation.org

To keep up with Erika and follow her journey, visit her Facebook page, *Moving Forward-Erika Brannock*: www.facebook.com/TheErikaBrannockFund